Miss Bindergarten Has a WILD DAY in Kindergarten

by **JOSEPH SLATE**

illustrated by **ASHLEY WOLFF**

PUFFIN BOOKS

PUFFIN BOOKS

Published by the Penguin Group

Penguin Young Readers Group, 345 Hudson Street, New York, New York 10014, U.S.A.

Penguin Group (Canada), 90 Eglinton Avenue East, Suite 700, Toronto, Ontario, Canada M4P 2Y3 (a division of Pearson Penguin Canada Inc.)

Penguin Books Ltd, 80 Strand, London WC2R 0RL, England

Penguin Ireland, 25 St Stephen's Green, Dublin 2, Ireland (a division of Penguin Books Ltd)

Penguin Group (Australia), 250 Camberwell Road, Camberwell, Victoria 3124, Australia (a division of Pearson Australia Group Pty Ltd)

Penguin Books India Pvt Ltd, 11 Community Centre, Panchsheel Park, New Delhi - 110 017, India

Penguin Group (NZ), Cnr Airborne and Rosedale Roads, Albany, Auckland 1310, New Zealand (a division of Pearson New Zealand Ltd)

Penguin Books (South Africa) (Pty) Ltd, 24 Sturdee Avenue, Rosebank, Johannesburg 2196, South Africa

Registered Offices: Penguin Books Ltd, 80 Strand, London WC2R 0RL, England

First published in the United States of America by Dutton Children's Books, a division of Penguin Young Readers Group, 2005
Published by Puffin Books, a division of Penguin Young Readers Group, 2006

15 14 13

Text copyright © Joseph Slate, 2005
Illustrations copyright © Ashley Wolff, 2005
All rights reserved

CIP Data is available.

Puffin Books ISBN 978-0-14-240709-7

Manufactured in China

For Marge Haganman, a teacher for over 42 years, who loves
the good days and laughs at the wild in Wapello. And to my
great-nephew Ensign Joe Sheridan—wild anchors aweigh.
J.S.

For Amy Whitcomb, who makes Miss Bindergarten look tame.
A.W.

Adam throws his hat too high.

Brenda bursts in late.

Christopher says he has to go—
he really cannot wait.

Miss Bindergarten begins

a wild day in kindergarten.

Danny tends his droopy beans.

Emily spies some ants.

Franny lifts her dress and shouts,
"I love my fancy pants!"

Miss Bindergarten has

a wild day in kindergarten.

Ian sadly tells Miss B,
"We didn't mean to tear."

Miss Bindergarten and the librarian

have a wild day in kindergarten.

Jessie drops the bug jar.

Miss Bindergarten and the nurse

have a wild day in kindergarten.

Matty checks a chrysalis.

Noah drops his rock.

Ophelia's oozy painting is sticking to her smock.

Patricia trips and flips her tray.

Quentin overloads.

Raffie Mack soaks **S**ara when his apple juice explodes.

Miss Bindergarten and the cafeteria helper

have a wild day in kindergarten.

Tommy dumps in too much dirt.

Ursula's seed pack rips.

Vicky pours in waaaaaaay too much, and the cardboard carton drips.

Now Miss Bindergarten and the custodian

have a wild day in kindergarten.

Wanda whacks the principal.

Miss Bindergarten and everyone enjoy

an even wilder day in kindergarten.

"**S**ometimes even a wild day," says Miss B, "turns up something wonderful to see."

Life cycle of a PLANT

Life cycle
of a
BUTTERFLY

LEAF

Milkweed

Caterpillar

Chrysalis

EGG

Butterfly

Adam · Alligator

Brenda · Beaver

Christopher · Cat

Danny · Dog

Emily · Elephant

Franny · Frog

Gwen · Gorilla

Henry · Hippopotamus

Ian · Iguana

Jessie · Jaguar

Kiki · Kangaroo

Lenny · Lion

Matty · Moose

Noah · Newt

Miss Bindergarten's
WILD DAY
Kindergarten

Ophelia · Otter

Patricia · Pig

Quentin · Quokka

Raffie · Rhinoceros

Sara · Squirrel

Tommy · Tiger

Ursula · Uakari monkey

Vicky · Vole

Wanda · Wolf

Xavier · Xenosaurus

Yolanda · Yak

Zach · Zebra

CoCo · Cockatoo

Miss Bindergarten **Mrs. Simpson** **Mr. King** **Mrs. Leo** **Nurse Nelson** **Ms. Chavez** **Carl Cox**
Border collie **Suricate** **Penguin** **Leopard** **Nyala** **Chimpanzee** **Coyote**